HANDTALK ZOO

TEN O'CLOCK!

GEORGE ANCONA & MARY BETH
FOUR WINDS PRESS, NEW YORK

WHERE

SHALL

WE

GO?

THERE!   THERE!   THERE!   THERE!   THERE!

Library of Congress Cataloging-in-Publication Data.   Ancona, George. Handtalk zoo / George Ancona and Mary Beth.—1st American ed.   p.   cm. Summary: Words and sign language depict children at the zoo discovering how to sign the names of various animals and how to tell time. ISBN 0-02-700801-0 (Macmillan) [1. Zoo animals—Fiction. 2. Deaf—Fiction. 3. Time—Fiction. 4. Clocks and watches—Fiction. 5. Sign language.] I. Mary Beth. II. Title. III. Title: Handtalk zoo. PZ7.A51874Han 1989   [Fic]—dc19 88-36861 CIP AC

ELEPHANT

BEAR!

TIGER

HORSE... WITH STRIPES (ZEBRA)

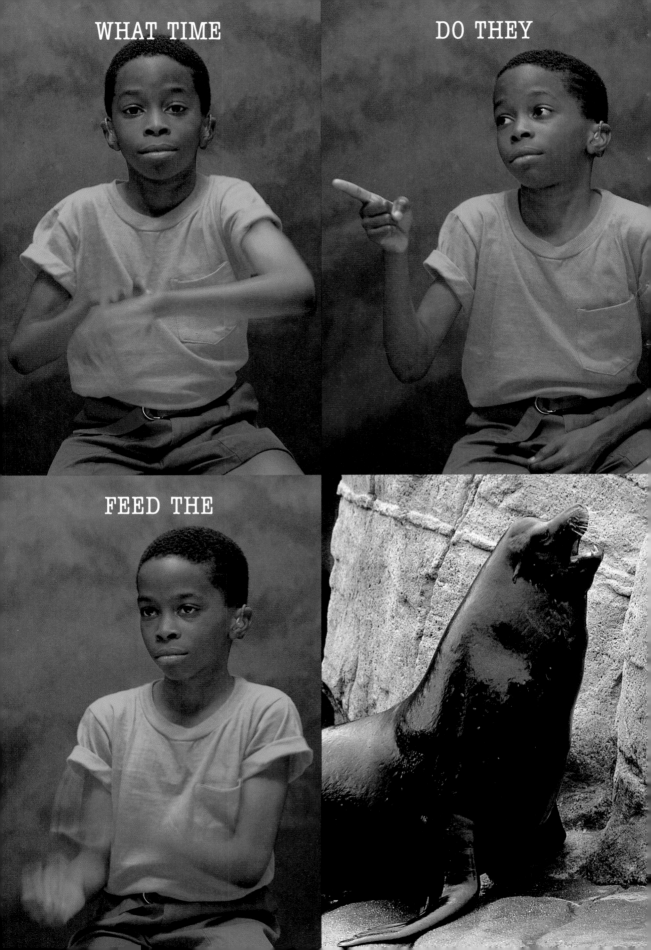

NOW!

I'M HUNGRY!

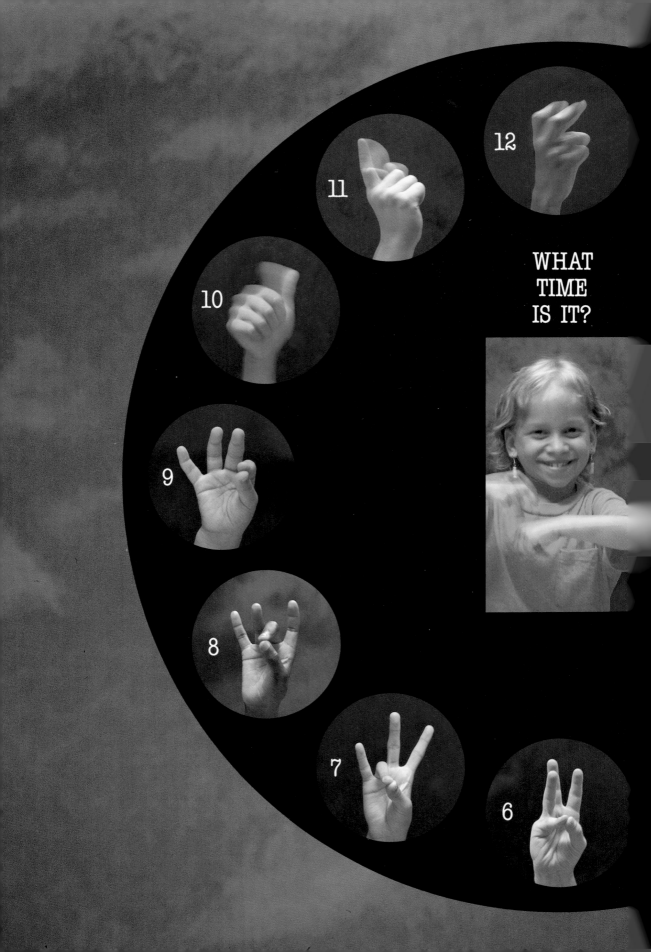

WHAT
TIME
IS IT?

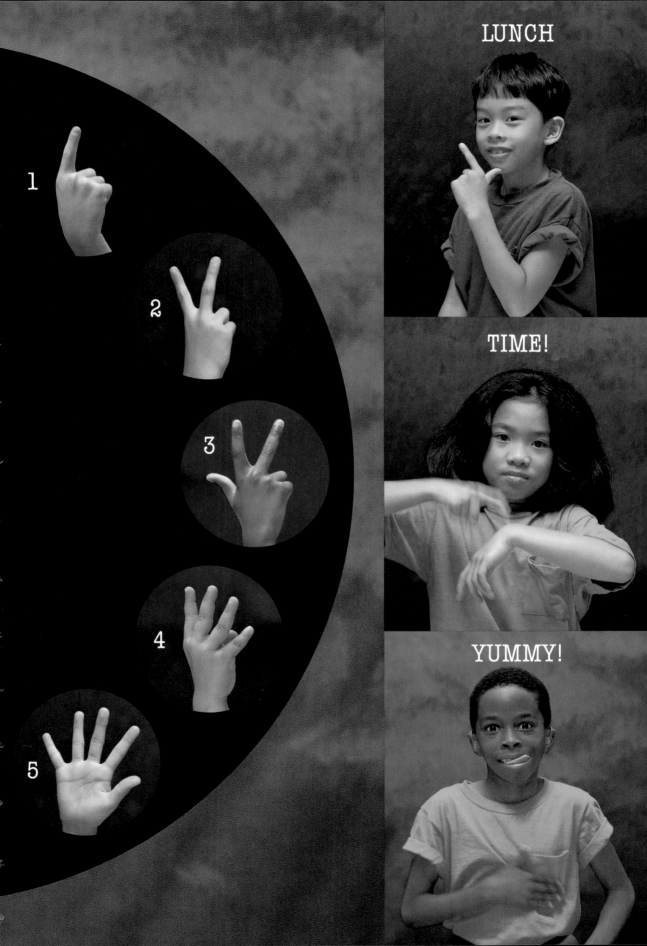

LUNCH

TIME!

YUMMY!

JUICE

MILK

PIZZA

POPCORN

HAMBURGER

ICE CREAM

APPLE

WHERE'S

ROGER?

COME DOWN!

YOU'RE

NOT A

MONKEY!

GIRAFFE

LION

CROCODILE

PARROT

DEER

WOLF

PENGUIN

WE Children's Zoo

CAN

TOUCH
THE

ANIMALS.

GOAT

DUCK

RABBIT

I'M TIRED. CLOSING TIME.

SO LONG!